SEAT #09

A haunted journey

ABUL HASAN

Seat #09

Publisher: Inkscribe Media Pvt. Ltd

ISBN Number: 978-1-966421-63-4

SEAT #09

It was a cold night in December 2023. Manas was going back to his hometown, Dibrugarh, Assam. He had taken a long leave from his busy schedule and work life. He had many plans and excitement, especially enjoying his mom's handmade food and chatting with his father, Mr. Mrinal Hazarika, a retired lieutenant from the Indian Army, and his childhood buddy Bikram Rajkhowa.

Manas wanted to live every moment of his vacation and have some nostalgic moments with his family as he would not be able to come for the next couple of years due to an upcoming project. Well, let me introduce Manas Hazarika.

He is an electrical and communication engineer and an IIT pass-out, 2018 batch, from IIT Kharagpur. After his final exams, Manas was selected by Alphabet Inc., popularly known as Google. Now an AI engineer, his current workstation is at Alphabet Inc., 1600 Amphitheatre Parkway in Mountain View, California.

Well, Manas's flight was delayed from Delhi to Guwahati late at night. When he checked, the next flight to Dibrugarh was the next day at 3 p.m. He got restless and called Bikram to book a bus ticket urgently. After a few minutes, Bikram booked a ticket on the Redbus app and asked him to board it from ISBT Guwahati. In a couple of hours, Manas reached the bus stand and boarded the bus. With lots of excitement, he settled his luggage and started listening to music. He noticed that seat no. 09 next to him was not occupied, and the bus started moving. He ignored it and lay back, looking outside the window. Slowly, he started dozing off as he was already exhausted due to the long journey.

After a couple of hours, the bus halted in Naharkatiya for dinner. One bus conductor poked him, and he woke up to have his dinner, as the bus would not stop for the next 5 hours. He had his dinner and lit a smoke. He noticed a beautiful girl standing next to him, busy with a phone conversation. He ignored her and moved onto his bus and grabbed his seat. To his surprise, the same girl came towards him and asked, "Excuse me, this seat no. is 26, right? I guess it's my seat. Would you give me some space to get in?" He reluctantly got off the seat and asked her to sit. She was wearing a soft and pleasant perfume, making him feel better. He thought, *Chalo! I will not be bored now.*

Manas was looking for an opportunity to talk to her..

But every time he looked at her face, she was wearing headphones and swiping her phone screen. They travelled for almost 3 hours when they heard a loud burst outside. The bus suddenly halted. People screamed from the front, "Ki hole?" "What happened?"

The conductor grinned and said not to worry; one of the tyres had burst. They were changing it, and it would take some time. If anybody had nature's call, they could go out and come back but were advised not to go far as it was a forest area. He just pushed himself to come out of the bus. A few minutes later, following him, the girl came out, filling his breath with her soft perfume. She stood near him and membaca, "Hello, how long will it take?" He replied, "Hi, I hope it will take 30 minutes, I guess." She said, "Oh, okay." He somehow managed the guts to ask her, "You are going to Dibrugarh, right?" She said yes, but she had to move to Lakhimpur from Dibrugarh. He said, "Okay." She then started a conversation, asking, "Are you from Dibrugarh?" "Yes, I am from Dibrugarh, now on a vacation, so going home." She said, "Oh, that's good to know." Then he asked her, "By the way, are you from Lakhimpur?" She replied,

"Yes, I have some work there, some old pending work. Will finish it and go back."

Manas relaxed and smiled with the thought, *The journey will be much better now.* He moved his hand forward and introduced himself, "Hi, I am Manas Hazarika, pleasure to meet you." She replied, "Hey, I am Nilakshi Baruah, same here, thanks."

The conductor signalled everyone to get onto the bus. Finally, it was back on its wheels now. He ushered her to take her seat, and they both settled for some time in silence. She asked him how often he visited home. He replied, "Once in a year." She said, "You must be very busy at work, I guess." He laughed, "Yes, at times, and also I stay far away from home, so you know it takes time." She looked at him and said, "Hmm, let me guess, you are a techie from Bangalore?" He replied, "The first part is true, but the second part is wrong." She asked, "What do you mean?" He said, "Yes, I am an AI engineer from California, USA." She replied, "Wow, that's cool." He asked her how she guessed he was a techie.

She smiled and said, with his powered glasses and restless attitude, she laughed. He was surprised by her observations and said, "Impressive." Soon their conversation was going at a good pace, with lots of discussion on politics, culture, and career. The bus halted near Jorhat, and the conductor asked everyone to go for a toilet break. He immediately decided to move out and release the pressure. When he came back, he found she was not on the bus. The driver started the bus. He screamed at the driver, "Wait, there is one passenger left behind!" The driver stopped the bus and recounted all the seats. He said all were in, but Manas told him a lady was sitting right beside him; where had she gone? The conductor smiled at him, ignored him, and moved into the driver's cabin. He was shocked at what was happening and why these people were so casual about a passenger.

He decided to check her luggage; it was not there. It was dark inside. The bus was moving at full speed. He could see fog outside, and it started getting cold. He decided to settle in his seat, and after some time, he got the same soft rosy smell. He turned around and saw the same lady standing next to him. He asked, "You? Where have you been?" She smiled and said she was sleeping in the back seat as it was empty, covered herself with the window's curtain, and laughed. She then asked him to give some space to sit next to him. He moved and looked at her with surprise.

She then asked him, "Hmm, worried about me? Huh?" He said, "Yes, I mean, of course, you are a co-passenger, so I was worried and afraid too. I thought you had missed the bus." She replied, "Okay, I am sorry, I was just kidding." She then asked him, "Am I married?" He asked her, "Do I look married?" She laughed, "Why, do married people look different or what?" He said, "No, but I am not married." He stopped any further conversation for a while and said, "It's personal, so I would rather not discuss this with you." She laughed and said, "Okay, never mind." He decided to keep silent for some time and pretended to fall asleep.

He could see the dawn lights coming from the east. It made him happy, and he was getting excited too as he was coming home and going to give a surprise to his mom. Then he saw on his right side she was sleeping. He decided not to disturb her. The conductor told them in 30 minutes they were arriving at their destination. He thought of waking her up. She opened her eyes all of a sudden and asked, "Ohh, you are leaving?" He said, "Yes, I am reaching home soon; my stoppage is a little early from the town." It was a pleasure to journey with you. He asked her, "Nilakshi, can I get your number, just to keep you in my friends' group?" She said, "I am sorry, I won't, but you can ping me on Instagram; I will message you." He smiled at her, took his luggage, and got down from the bus. She waved from the window with a smile and wished him a happy vacation. The bus left towards Dibrugarh ISBT. It was early at 5 a.m. He found an auto and reached home.

He could feel the fresh air in his house's front yard garden—what a beautiful day. He rang the bell. His mother came out half-asleep and screamed, "Ahh, Manas, my son," and hugged him. He too hugged her tight and kissed her forehead, saying, "Maa, tuk bor miss korisilu" ("Mother, I missed you a lot"). After a while, he unpacked his luggage and got a beautiful silk sari in maroon colour; maroon is his mother's favourite colour.

The next day, as planned, he had his favourite breakfast, bora saul and gur (sticky rice and jaggery), then moved out to their backyard, which was full of greenery. He called Bikram. They started fishing at their pond and having discussions on life and culture. Bikram used to ask him many questions about American life and his work culture. He told him, even though he had so many facilities at work, he still missed his home every night. He told him, especially his mom and dad. Bikram said, "I know that, bro." So, what's next? Any plans for marriage, or have you already chosen some firangi (foreigner)?

He laughingly said, "Not yet, bro, but yes, someone just touched my heart while I was on my way home." Bikram said, "Hmm, who is she?" "A very ecstatic and strange girl; her name is Nilakshi." Bikram said, "Cool, then how about meeting her?" He told him, "Bro, she was reluctant to share her phone number and asked me to message her on Instagram instead." Bikram said, "Let's find her on Instagram and make contact." He pulled out his cell phone and started finding her on Instagram. There were a dozen Nilakshis that popped out, but none were matching her face. He urged him, "Bro, leave it now; let's go on a drive to Dibrugarh town." How is Phukan sir, our math tuition sir? Bikram, with a sad expression, said, "Hey, bro, sorry to tell you, he passed away last year due to a cardiac arrest." "Oh, I am so sorry to hear that; may his soul rest in peace."

Eventually, both he and Bikram went to the town to hang out. While they were crossing the Chowkiding rail line, he saw a girl staring and smiling at him. To his surprise, it was Nilakshi. He waved to her, "Hey! How are you? What are you doing here?" She smiled and replied she was at her aunt's house for a day and would leave for North Lakhimpur tomorrow. "Oh, great! I could not find you on Instagram, though. Hope you will message me. Bye now." Then he left. Bikram looked at him during the entire conversation and told him, "Who did you talk and wave to now?" "Hey, didn't you see? It was Nilakshi." Bikram asked him to halt the car and said, "Bro, trust me, there was no one at that spot; rather, I saw an old rag-picking lady you were talking to." He laughed at him and asked him to go to an eye doctor and do a test. Then, happily, they moved on. They waited at a restaurant, and Bikram was looking at him weirdly. He then asked him the entire story of how he met her.

He then asked him to go back to their home. Bikram looked into his eyes and asked, "Brother, you need some rest. I will talk to you tomorrow morning." Then he left. Later that evening, he had a great time with his parents. They were watching Assamese TV serials with a cup of tea and some homemade pitha (cake). After having dinner, he went to his bed and took out his cell phone. There were many unanswered emails from his company. Some of his clients were not aware that he was on leave, so he informed them. Later, before sleeping, he was thinking of Nilakshi, and her laugh was buzzing in his ears. He started browsing her name on Instagram and Facebook. He found a weird name, $nilblueeye$. He guessed this must be Nilakshi's; like her character, she had also kept a strange name. So, with lots of curiosity and doubts, he messaged her with a "Hi."

In a few moments, he dozed off and was not aware of where he kept his phone. In his dream, he saw a weird place where Nilakshi was running hard, and some strange people with dark faces were chasing her. From the other side, where he was standing, she hugged him tight. All the people chasing her disappeared. Nilakshi looked into his eyes, and he saw a blaze of fire in her eyes.

Suddenly, his door was knocked, and his whole body was shivering. It was his mother who came into his room and woke him up. "Baba, utha, deri hoise" ("Dear son, wake up, it's getting late"), let's get to the temple.

When his mother touched his forehead, he had a high fever. Checked with a thermometer, it was reading 102 degrees. She got worried and asked him to take a rest. Then, from the other corner of his room, she gave him a paracetamol and asked him to have it after breakfast. He saw some red marks on his neck, and it was paining. He was wondering how these marks had come. After their breakfast, he was feeling much better. His mother told him, due to a change of water and air, his body must have been affected. "It's okay, you will be fine in a few days." In an hour, his father came to his room and asked him to dress up. He asked why. He told them they were going to Moran to meet Mr. Dinesh Baruah, an old colleague of his, who had invited them for lunch. His mother asked if they should take him with them because he was not well. He told his mother it was okay; he would feel better if he moved out. His parents later agreed, and all three moved for Moran. On the way, he could see mesmerizing views of tea gardens and greenery everywhere.

After 3 hours of journey, they finally reached Moran town. They called Baruah's uncle to guide them to his home address, and after a few struggles, they managed to reach his house. It was an old British-style bungalow surrounded by gardens everywhere—an impressive campus he loved. Mr. Baruah came forward and took them to his guest room and asked them to freshen up. Outside the window, he saw a young lady screaming at a little boy. He laughed at her and moved to the drawing room.

Mr. Baruah started calling, "Khewali... Khewali, look who has come." That girl ran inside the room, saw them, and greeted them with a smile. Dinesh's uncle introduced her as his youngest daughter, just come home from Delhi to do her Master's at Hindu College. With a hello and shy smile, she moved inside her room. After a while, Mrs. Baruah and Khewali came to the dining room with some snacks and tea. While enjoying the snacks, both Mr. Hazarika and Mr. Baruah started telling their old stories during their initial days in army training, sharing many funny incidents. All started laughing loudly.

While they were talking, he decided to take a break and asked for the restroom. Uncle Baruah guided him towards the toilet. Later, he decided to take a stroll in their garden, which was beautiful and had many exotic flowers. While he was taking some pictures of these flowers, he could feel someone standing behind him. It was none other than Khewali; she was smiling at him. He greeted her and appreciated the way they had maintained their garden with so many beautiful and rare flowers. Khewali replied, "It's all done by my parents; they have a common hobby of gardening. They used to visit remote places to collect these flower seeds. At times, they used to order from Burma also."

He was impressed. Later, they started discussing their professions. Khewali was doing her Master's in Physics from Hindu College, New Delhi, and would be going back in a week. He also shared some memories of his in Delhi while he was doing his graduation. He used to visit Delhi IIT to meet his friends; they used to party hard. She appreciated Google and its innovations. Khewali later asked about his daily life in California. Eventually, they both had a good time and were in conversation for quite a long time. Before they could go on and on, he could hear his mother calling him and Khewali for lunch. Mrs. Baruah had cooked all Assamese ethnic cuisine; it was too yummy and mesmerizing. She is a good cook. He especially liked the duck curry with colocasia stem (kosur thari).

Later in the evening, they had a cup of tea and decided to leave for Dibrugarh as it was getting dusk. Khewali shook his hand and said, "So, Mr. Manas, it was nice meeting you. Can I get your number, just to keep in touch?" They exchanged their numbers and left from Moran. While returning, he was driving the car. During the entire journey, his father was only praising Mrs. Baruah's cooking. He could see his mom was fuming at him and said, "Hmm, as if I don't know cooking. You better stay at Mr. Baruah's house from tomorrow; I won't cook anything for you." Looking at their childish behaviour, he was laughing like anything. He said, "Both of you, now be silent; both of you are disturbing my driving with your squirrel quarrels." He smiled at his mom.

Later that night, before going to bed, he was checking his phone. A message popped up: "Have you reached home safe?" It was Khewali. With a smile, he answered, "Yes, thanks," then replied, "It was a lovely day, and thanks for your company; else I would have been bored." She replied with thanks and good night. While he was about to sleep, he could see the windows of his room were wide open, so he decided to close them. Far at a distance, he saw a dark humanoid figure watching him. He got scared and called his mother. She came rushing to his room. He asked her, "Mom, I just saw a dark figure roaming around our garden." Mom smiled at him and said, "You must be very tired; go to your bed and sleep now." Then she moved towards the window and said, "There is no one. Oh, it could be our neighbour's mad son who often crosses their boundary wall and moves around. Just ignore it now and sleep."

While he was about to sleep, he could hear the loud sound of the window of his room banging and opening again, as if someone had opened it forcefully. He could feel the wind was blowing faster and faster. It was a very spooky situation. He decided not to go near the window. He pulled up his blanket, hid his face, and slept off. He woke up early in the morning and immediately rushed towards the window. He saw his mom was plucking flowers for her puja. He immediately rushed to her and checked the place where he saw someone last night. He saw a mark on their mango tree; it was a mark of nail scratching. He asked his mother, "Mom, look at it; what mark could it be?" Mom very casually touched his forehead and said, "Son, it could be street dogs who visit our home at night for food. What is wrong with you? Why do you look so panicky? You do not behave like this before."

With a quavering voice, he said, "Mom, I am fine; just had a bad dream last night." Later that day, he was only thinking about the haunted images he saw, but no one believed him. So he decided to call Bikram to discuss it. He also laughed at him and told him, "Brother, I don't mind; I seriously think you need a psychiatrist. I could feel you are getting hallucinated ever since you have come—first that lady Nilakshi, now a dark image."

Bikram told him he had a plan: "Let's go to my home; tonight you will be staying with me and be my guest." He agreed to it and left for his home, which is a few meters away from his house. He had a great time with him that evening. Bikram took out his old pics with him in school; it was nostalgic, and then they cracked jokes about their old mates. After dinner, they both went to bed. After a while,

Bikram asked him, "Aren't you missing Nilakshi?" He replied, "Yes, but she is not contacting me. I have not even received any reply to my 'hi' on Instagram. No idea, bro." After a long chat, they slept at 1 a.m., but he experienced something really strange. He saw the same old dream where Nilakshi was running to him and hugged him with eyes of fire. Then he woke up. Bikram was also awake at that time. He asked him, "What happened?" He told him, "The same old dream of Nilakshi is annoying me now. Now I feel there is some connection between me and Nilakshi."

Bikram told him he would take him to a baba tomorrow, a very famous baba near the old Shiv temple, and ask him if any witch has an eye on him. But he, being anti-superstition, was reluctant. Rather, he thought of going online and consulting with a psychiatrist. Later, the next morning, Bikram forced him to go to the old Shiv temple and introduced him to Baba Kaushik. He was a skinny old man with a long beard; he was looking very strangely towards him. Bikram asked him, "Baba, you seem disturbed. What is the issue? Why are you looking at Manas like this?" Baba was quiet for some time and said something was following him, and now it is waiting for and watching them from a distance.

Bikram and Manas got goosebumps and started looking at each other. They asked Baba to tell them what it was. Baba said, "She is a witch who targets young men and makes them her prey. As time passes, she will reveal herself to both of you." Bikram angrily asked why. What had they done? Baba, with a worried face, said, "It's someone's bad karma; now others are facing her vengeance." He asked both of them to come after sunset so that he could do a yagna and tell the entire story. He requested them to take a rudraksha seed from his temple and keep it with them, which will protect them from bad spirits, and asked them to leave now. Manas and Bikram held each other's hands and left that temple.

While going home, both were in absolute silence. Suddenly, Manas's phone rang; it was his mother, who asked him to come soon; someone was waiting to have lunch with him.

Manas worriedly asked, "Who is it, Mother?" She told him, "I won't tell you; come home fast." Both Manas and Bikram rushed to their home and found it was Khewali who was waiting for them. Manas greeted Khewali and asked her what made her visit his home. She told him, "Nothing special; I had some work at Dibrugarh University. My mom asked me to visit your home to give you this African Queen Lily plant; Aunty had requested it from your last visit." With a smile of gratitude, Manas requested her to join them for lunch. While having lunch, Bikram was very shy in front of Khewali. Manas noted that and introduced Bikram to her and requested her to have some more chicken curry and not to be shy.

After lunch, they all had a good chat about flowers and gardening. Khewali also appreciated their rose garden and promised to give some more yellow rose plants on her next visit. She had to leave for her home as she was going to Delhi in a couple of days to continue her classes. While leaving, she told Manas that she would call him from Delhi and smiled. Bikram also smiled and waved at her, grinning cheerfully. Manas asked, "Hmm, what's cooking, brother?" Bikram made a coy face and ignored it.

Later that evening, while Manas was about to sleep, he got a phone call with no number displaying. He immediately picked up the call. He heard a lady's voice; it was Nilakshi. She told Manas, "It's been a long time; I can feel that you are remembering me. So I thought of calling you." Manas asked her, "How did you get my number?" She told him, "From a reference; I won't tell his name. Leave it; when can I meet you?" Manas reluctantly told her, "I am busy now; I will inform you, but I can't see your number reflecting on my phone. How can I call you?" She laughed and said, "It's a secret." She said, "I know someone else is occupying your mind, and you do not miss me anymore." Manas asked, "Why would I miss you? You were just a co-passenger for a few hours." Nilakshi said, "But I saw something else in your eyes." She requested Manas to meet. "If you do not come, I will be hurt; please meet me at DU park tomorrow at 2 p.m." Manas called Bikram immediately and talked about the phone incident. He asked him to wait for him and said he would meet him in the evening. Bikram came at 5 p.m. and asked Manas not to go there; he could sense some danger lurking around him.

Later that night, while he was sleeping, he saw Nilakshi in his dream kissing him intensely. He woke up suddenly; he could see a dark image staring at him, standing right beside his bed. He screamed out of fear. His mother rushed to his room and asked what happened. Manas was so afraid that he was numb and unable to utter anything for some time. Then he told the entire story of Nilakshi and seeing dark shadows ever since he met her. His mother got scared and decided to do a Sani Puja at their home in the morning. The purohit came and did Sani Puja, but he told his mother that he could sense negative energy in their house, but after this puja, it would vanish. His mother, with a smile of relief, thanked the purohit and offered him lunch. She asked him to distribute prasad to their neighbours, so Manas left with Bikram to distribute prasad.

On the way, Bikram told Manas to keep the rudraksha seed with him; it would protect him from evil forces. Manas worriedly said that since he was not going to meet Nilakshi today, would there be any other consequences he would face? Bikram decided to meet Kaushik Baba for help and suggestions. He asked Manas to stay at home, and he would meet him in the evening.

That day, Bikram met Kaushik Baba, who told him that Manas's life was in danger, and that witch was behind him, and she wanted to kill Manas. Bikram asked Baba, "How can we

stop it?" Kaushik Baba said that a witch needs moksha (freedom). She is on revenge. You have to trace the history of the girl Nilakshi, how she died, and bring the culprit in front of her. She kills the person who falls in love with her as she was betrayed by someone; later, she was gang-raped and killed by the person whom she loved. Then Bikram asked Baba, "When did this incident happen?" Baba closed his eyes and said, "This incident happened 5 years ago in a North Lakhimpur tea garden." Since then, every year, she targets one man with whom she pretends to fall in love.

Manas was very sad that day after knowing about Nilakshi. He decided to go to the root of it and punish the culprits, but it was not as easy as it seemed. A few days later, Manas and Bikram decided to meet Kaushik Baba to get some details of Nilakshi. Kaushik Baba, since he is a tantric and with his spiritual power, Manas would get the details or direction of the exact location where the incident happened. Baba Kaushik called them to his temple in the evening and asked them to go to the temple pond to take a bath and sit beside him. It was evening time, around 5 p.m., and darkness surrounded everywhere. Baba Kaushik brought a lamp and a plate with mustard oil on it. He started chanting mantras. Manas started getting goosebumps, and he could feel the burning flesh smell around him. Baba Kaushik's eyes became red, and he was making weird noises. Bikram started getting panicky; he held his hand tight. After a few minutes, Baba was asking a dark shadow standing right in front of them to know the location where Nilakshi died. The plate with mustard oil started shaking, and suddenly the oil surface showed images of the incident and the culprits' faces. Then, on the sand, the place's name appeared: "Bihpuriya." In a moment, Baba fainted, and the lamp light turned off. The dark shadow slowly receded away in the darkness, and Manas screamed out in fear. Both Manas and Bikram ran away from that place and moved to their homes.

On 10th December 2024, both Manas and Bikram went to a small village called Bihpuriya, situated in the Lakhimpur District of Assam. They decided to visit the nearest police station to get any information about Nilakshi's case. Mr. Bora, head constable of Bihpuriya P.S., asked them how he might help them. Manas narrated the story of Nilakshi that happened 5 years ago in a North Lakhimpur tea garden. Mr. Bora paused for a moment and asked them to wait. Then, after 20 minutes, he brought a dusty file, which had the investigation report of Nilakshi's death. In the report, it was mentioned that she was raped and her throat cut by 5 unknown men. Due to those huge dharnas erupted by social workers and localities, the matter was escalated to the CM's office. Eventually, the case was moved to CID, but after a couple of months, investigation on this case had been stopped due to some confidential reasons, and the final report is still pending in this case.

Manas found it very disturbing and asked why it was still pending. Why, after 5 years, were the culprits still moving free? Mr. Bora said, "Ki kobo aru, anekuwai soli thake" ("What to do, things are like this only"). Very disappointing to know how the system works. Mr. Bora came a little closer and asked to meet him at the outside tea stall. In a while, Mr. Bora came to meet them and said, "I could not tell you a few things in the PS, but the fact is one of the culprits was Nilakshi's boyfriend, who promised her to get married, but he is the son of our local MLA. He somehow duped her and raped her with his friends. The MLA has given a huge amount of money to keep the matter silent. But I am feeling very sad for the poor girl; my condolences are always with Nilakshi." And he left.

Manas decided to stay in Bihpuriya and go to her family to learn more about the case. Manas took Nilakshi's home address from the police file and asked Bikram to take a rickshaw. Eventually, they went to her village named Phul. After reaching Nilakshi's home, he noticed the home was surrounded by thick bushes and a half-constructed RCC building near her home. The place was very silent; at a distance, a middle-aged old lady was watering the garden. He called her, "Baidew, eikhon Nilakhir ghor hoi neki baru?" ("Hello, sister, is it Nilakshi's house?") That lady stopped for a moment and came towards Manas running. "Are you from the police? Will she get justice?" With tears in her eyes, "Bupai, kun hoi tohot?" ("Who are you, son?") Manas told her, "Baidew, I am Manas from Dibrugarh, and he is Bikram, my friend." That lady called both of them inside her house, asked them to sit, and offered tea. While having tea, Manas told the entire story to her mother, Nilima Choudhury. Her mother held his hand and cried like a child. She told him, "Son, my daughter was cheated by Diganta Hazarika, son of MLA Kishor Hazarika. Ever since she left us, we are broken. The pain of her loss could not be tolerated by her father; even he left me last year due to a heart attack. Now I am living all alone in pain and agony. Nilakshi's father has left some pension money for me; that's the only hope for my survival now."

Her mother told him Nilakshi was a very fun-loving and joyful girl; she always wanted to live her life in her way. Being their only child, they had also given all privileges to her. She was very interested in doing modelling, but her father was reluctant and rejected her request; rather, he asked her to focus on her studies. She was admitted to Dibrugarh University.

During her 1st semester in 2019, she was ranked first in an inter-college modelling competition. After, she got many offers for modelling shows. At the parties, she met Diganta Hazarika, and very soon they became good friends. There were many occasions when he visited their home with a police escort to pick up their daughter for shows and parties. In her heart, she was a little happy and proud too that such a big man's son was after her daughter. She even told her husband that Diganta was a nice guy and, if Nilakshi got married to him, he could keep her happy. But somewhere, her husband was not happy with these ongoing talks and gossiping in the town, and he said that they had given half their life to bring up their child and to shape her future, but he was afraid things were slipping out of his hand. On 15th November 2021, Nilakshi called her in the afternoon from Guwahati that she had to leave for Mumbai urgently for an audition and would come back in 5-7 days. That was the last call she had heard from her, and after a pause, Nilima Baidew sobbed out and said, after 2 days, they found her dead body with cuts and burns in a tea garden near their house. They all were silent for a while. Bikram came forward and consoled Nilima Baidew, "Please don't cry; we are here to help you. As I know, we cannot bring her back, but we can give her justice and put the culprits behind bars." Her mother said, "I believe God must have sent both of you for this." She later requested both of them to stay that night in their house. Manas agreed to it, but Bikram was a little worried that Nilakshi's spirit doesn't like it. But Manas told him, "Don't worry; even her spirit understands that we are there to help her."

The next morning, when Manas woke up, he could feel the same perfume which he felt on his first meeting. He took some of her pictures from an old album secretly and asked Bikram to get ready as they had to leave. After morning breakfast, Manas said, "Dear Baideo (sister), please take care of yourself; we will find out the culprit and give justice to her. Now we have to go, but you can call me at this number if you get any information. Oh, please do not inform anyone that we are investigating this case."

While on the way, Manas looked at his calendar, and he hardly had one more week to go as he was going to finish his holidays. He said, "Bikram, we need to work fast to find out the culprits and make them confess before Nilakshi takes any other life." In a while, he got Khewali's call: "Hi, Manas, how are you? No news? Have you forgotten me?" Manas, with a smile, said, "No, why would I? Just busy with some work." Khewali was coming back to Moran for a few days as Baruah's uncle was not well. Manas said, "Hey, Khewali, can I meet you for a few hours? I need to tell you something." Khewali, excited, said, "Sure, you can, but I won't be able to give you much time. Once I reach Dibrugarh Airport, I will call you."

Bikram, with a naughty smile, asked Manas, "Hmm, what's up, buddy? Your face is charming now." Manas told him, "Leave it, bro. Let's go to see Diganta's house and get some information." Bikram said, "I am wondering why Nilakshi has not attacked Diganta till now and killed innocent people who do not have any business with her." Manas told him, "Nilakshi might have attempted; we will only come to know once we start inquiring about him from the localities."

After reaching Bihpuriya town, they went to Diganta's house and pretended to be his old lost friends from Dibrugarh University. One security man from the main gate took their details and requested them to wait. After some time, one other person came from inside and asked them to come in. He took them to the lawn and asked them to sit. It was a beautifully decorated bungalow with gardens everywhere. After a while, an old man came out and was introduced as Mr. Kishor Hazarika, ex-MLA. They both stood up and greeted him. He asked them to tell him who they were and how he could help them. Manas said they were Diganta's college friends and had just gotten to know his house, so they came in to meet him. That old man was looking very strangely at both of them and kept staring at them for some time and asked, "When did you meet him for the last time?" Manas quickly answered, "About 2-3 years back in Dibrugarh at a party." The man paused, "Don't you know that he died 3 years ago in a car accident? And with him, 3 of his other friends also died."

Manas and Bikram stumbled for a moment and stood up. "I am sorry to know; I guess that's why we found his phone number does not exist when I tried calling him a year ago." Mr.

Kishor asked them to sit and bring their heads forward and tell them, "You can't lie and never do it in future. Since you both are like my son's age, I am leaving you now. Next time, I hope I won't see your faces near my campus, else I will shoot both of you." With a frowning eye, he looked at them and left. Manas and Bikram both looked confused and walked out silently from that campus. They both decided to have a cup of tea and discuss the matter. Bikram said, "Now I understand what Nilakshi wants is the truth to come out, which will break the fake ego of Mr. Kishor Hazarika." Later that evening, after asking a few questions about Diganta, the tea stall guy said, "Our Diganta babu was a very good man, but he was cheated on by a girl from Phul Bagan village, and one day, eventually, out of heavy drinking, he and his friends died on the spot." Since then, many young guys have been killed in the same spot. People do not drive through that area alone at night. Bikram got goosebumps because even they had to pass through the same road; it's Dhemaji to Dibrugarh road near Kulajan. Bikram told Manas, "Let's somehow reach Lakhimpur and halt for tonight." But while they were discussing hotel rooms in Lakhimpur, Manas's father rang him. While receiving the call, "Son, where are you? Please come home as early as you can; your mother is behaving abnormally different and changing her voice, calling your name. Please come home; I have called the doctor." Manas told Bikram, "We have to rush to our home; Mother is not well." Bikram immediately started their car and headed towards Dibrugarh. While on the way, Manas called their maid, Rahima Bai, "Bai, what happened?" Bai said, "Don't ask me; your mother has been possessed by some kind of ghost. She has been hitting herself and making weird noises. I am very afraid; please bring our temple pujari; he is a tantric while coming."

Manas rushed to his home with Pandit Kaushik. When they went near his mother, she made a growling voice and looked at Manas. She then uttered, "Baiman... Baiman. Moi tuk eri najau... tuk moi loi jam... hahahahaha" ("You betrayer, I will not leave you; I will take you with me," then she laughed). Immediately after that, Manas's mother fainted and fell.

Tantric Kaushik silently watched everything and told them, "Your family members are in danger. That spirit has entered your home and will take a life before Amavasha (no-moon night)." They all lifted his mother and took her to a bed and asked her, "Mother, how are you?" She told him, "I saw a dark tall shadow standing near me; before I could scream, it entered my body through my mouth. Then I don't remember what I did. Son, what is happening? What was it?" Tantric Kaushik narrated the entire story to Manas's mother. She cried loudly after listening to it, "Why is that devil behind my only son?" Then she told Baba Kaushik, "Please help us; give us a solution."

Baba Kaushik then did meditation in Manas's room and said the only way to escape from Nilakshi's spirit was by staying at home for 7 days till the no-moon night. "I will chant a protective mantra on mustard seeds and will make a line circumferent of your house; it will protect Manas. But make sure Manas does not cross the line." Both Manas, Bikram, and Mother agreed to it. Baba Kaushik gave one rudraksha seed to Manas's mother for her protection and left from that place. Later that night, Bikram, out of fear, stayed at Manas's home. The next day, Manas's mother was feeling better but had a severe headache.

Manas's mother requested Bikram, "Son, do visit us daily as you know Manas is restricted to go out." Bikram said, "Sure, aunty, do not worry; I will be visiting Manas, and please let me know for any help." With a smile, Bikram left.

Later, after a couple of days, Khewali called Manas. It was a normal hi call, but listening to Manas's low tone, Khewali asked what happened. Manas narrated the entire story to her. For a moment, Khewali got shivers and panicked. She told him, "I am sorry to know about it, but why have you kept it hidden from me all this while?" Manas told her, "I did not want to bother you for that as I knew you would get panicked." Khewali told him, "Don't worry; things will be fine; do what Baba Kaushik instructed you to do. I may come to Moran for a few days as my project is over; I will spend some time at home. However, I may come to your home." Manas replied, "Okay, sure, please come; I also have to extend my leave from work."

After 5 days, on 9th Jan 2024, Khewali called Manas that she was on the way to Dibrugarh and would visit their home. After a few hours, Khewali was standing at the gate of Manas, but she screamed out loud as she was chased by a stray dog. Listening to her scream, Manas ran out to save her, but during that process, he made a grave mistake; he crossed the protection line of Baba Kaushik and went out of it.

Both came inside the home, but a chilling breeze came inside their home, and the window curtain started fluttering wildly. Khewali said, "The weather was sunny a few minutes ago; how come I am feeling so chill in your room, and why is the wind blowing so fast?" Manas stopped for a while, then screamed, "Oh shit! I made a mistake; I crossed that line made by Baba Kaushik. Oh my God, what am I going to do now?" Khewali, "You are not safe here; please go to your home immediately; I have to call the Tantric Baba Kaushik now." He immediately called Bikram, told him about the incident, and asked him to bring Baba Kaushik. After an hour, Bikram told Manas, "I am sorry; Baba Kaushik is out of town; he went for a tirth yatra (pilgrimage journey)." Bikram rushed to their home, took Khewali, and dropped her to the bus stand.

In the evening, Manas was sitting in his room with his mother when suddenly they heard a banging noise on their roof. Then the windows and doors started closing and opening very hard; mirrors started breaking. Manas's mother screamed out in fear. Manas's father came to his room with his 9mm licensed pistol and shouted, "Whoever it is, come forward!" Since Manas's father was a brave man, as he was a soldier in the Indian Army.

Soon, Manas got a phone call from Khewali's mother: "What have you done to my daughter? She is behaving very weirdly; her voice has changed, and she is banging her head on the wall, screaming your name. What is happening to her? Is she possessed by some evil? Oh, Ram, hai Krishna, what will happen now?" In a blink, Khewali's face changed to Nilakshi's face.

Khewali's mother screamed, and her phone got disconnected.

Manas started shivering, and he fell down on the floor, and he started screaming, "She is coming... she is coming; someone please help me." On the other side, Nilakshi was telling, "Today I will take Manas; my promise is going to be over. Your daughter has started loving Manas, hahaha... I won't let it happen. I have been betrayed by men; I will not let this happen to Khewali."

Manas's mother called Bikram; he rushed to Manas's room and brought a doctor. When the doctor held Manas's hand, he was kicked out of the door; the doctor got fainted immediately. Then a call came from an unknown number; it was Baba Kaushik from the other side. Baba

Kaushik told them, "I know what is happening; since I am out of home, please switch on the phone speaker, put it on a glass of water. I am going to chant some holy mantras; sprinkle it on Manas's body; the evil will leave his body now. And there is one more lady who is Manas's friend; call that lady's mother; put me on conference." Likewise, the mantras were chanted by Tantric Baba. After a while, both Manas and Khewali calmed down but were unconscious. Baba Kaushik said, "Though it is silent now, it is not over yet. I am coming soon; till then, you keep sprinkling this holy water on both of them. I have to do a yagna at your home to give moksha to this evil spirit."

The very next day, a Muslim saint person visited their home to get some food. He was staring at the doors and said to Manas's mother, "Daughter, if I am not wrong, there is some negative energy in your home. Something is wrong or going to be wrong. Is everything alright?" Manas's mother told the story. Listening to it, the saint person told her, "Allah will guide you. Can I come inside and sit for a while?" Manas's mother greeted him and offered him a glass of water and some food. That saint person said that their son had been possessed by a devil named "Vetala"; it possesses a human body and kills them. He then took out a ring from his bag and gave it to her. He said, "It is a very powerful gem; it has many holy prayers; ask your son to wear it. He will be protected." Then the saint person gave his mobile number and told her for any help and not to be reluctant to call him and left. In the evening, Baba Kaushik told them that he was in Guwahati and would be reaching Dibrugarh by tonight. He would be starting his puja tomorrow morning and also requested to bring Khewali to their home for exorcism.

As planned, all arrived at Manas's home. Baba Kaushik then said that in his absence, a Muslim saint person had come to their home, right? Mother responded, "Yes, please call him also." On 13th Jan 2025, morning, all had come and gathered near Baba Kaushik. Baba Kaushik asked to bring a black goat alive; through mantra, the devil's spirit would be put inside the goat's body, and they would sacrifice it in the name of God to get rid of this evil soul. The Muslim saint person said he would also recite some powerful surahs from the Quran Sharif to throw back this evil spirit. At 4:30 p.m., the day was near to dusk time. Both Manas and Khewali were tied tightly with ropes to the house pillar, and the fire yagna was made between them, surrounded with lights, diyas, and candles.

Tantric Kaushik started chanting mantras, and the Muslim saint person started reciting the Holy Book, the Quran Sharif. After a moment, all diyas and candles were blown off by a cold breeze, as if the evil had come inside their home. Both Manas and Khewali started shaking their heads with their eyes popping out and making growling noises like dogs. The rest of the people were holding each other tight and watching everything from the other room with the doors closed. A dark shadow stood in front of them and narrated her story with pain and grief.

Baba Kaushik told the evil, "Why are you taking the life of innocent people? What is their fault in it?" Nilakshi's ghost told him she started liking Manas, and whoever came in between, she would kill them. Then the shadow vanished, and Khewali was crying and laughing at the same moment and said, "I am in love with Manas; I will take him to my world." Manas was watching all of this with fear on his face and was crying out loudly.

But Baba Kaushik made a trick. He said, "Yes, you can, but first you have to show me your power; now enter any living creature's body except human beings." Nilakshi's ghost said, "I am a Vetala; I can enter anyone's body." Then Baba Kaushik asked her to prove it! In no time, the goat started talking like a human: "I am inside him." Immediately, Baba Kaushik held the goat upside down and slit its throat and threw it in the burning flame of the yagna and chanted the mantra of moksha of the evil soul. The goat was screaming horrifyingly, and in a while, the locked door was kicked open with force. Both Khewali and Manas fainted and fell down on the ground.

Baba Kaushik stood up and said the evil had left their home, but it was a dark shadow; it would not come as long as they kept Manas away from this town. He gave some mustard seeds and asked to throw them around their house. The Muslim saint said, "I will pray to Allah to protect this house," and gave a tabiz to Manas and Khewali to wear; it would protect them from evil spirits.

Soon after this horrific incident, Manas left for the USA and joined his job, and Khewali also moved out from Moran and settled in Mumbai, joining an IT company. Bikram opened a showroom in Dibrugarh. Almost everyone was settled. Manas and Khewali proposed to each other, and their families also agreed to tie their knot soon. After a year, Manas came back home, and as planned, both got married happily with lots of blessings from their family and friends. Khewali moved with Manas to the USA.One day Manas had to go to New Jersey for an official visit later that evening after talkingto Khewali

Manas was scrolling his old photo suddenly he found some old pictures with Bikram he smiled and checked his watch it was 12 AM in India Manas called Bikaram .Bikram on the other side was driving to North Lakhimpur for a bussiness work he sounded busy but he managed to talk for a while but he said to Manas bro I have to tell you something not now , something is wrong ..then he said will call later brother busy in driving then he hung up the call . When Manas was talking to Bikram ,He felt two red glowing eyes were watching him from the other side of his hotel window. Manas ignored it and called the room service to clean the room just to be with a company in his room for a while .

After couple of days , while reading Assam Tribune online, Manas's eyes locked on an article: a young

man named Bikram Das found dead near Lakhimpur-Dibrugarh highway. He knew it was late night in India, but still, he called out to his dad. "Dad, is the news right?" His dad cried and told him, "Yes, son,

Bikram has lost his life; he met with an accident in NH 15 near Kulajan." Manas broke down and screamed out, "Nooo!! Why, God? That bitch has taken my best friend's life." Both Khewali and Manas wanted to come to Dibrugarh to do his last rites, but they were stopped by Manas's mother: "Son, remember Baba Kaushik asked you to stay away from Dibrugarh. You do not worry; he is like my son too; we all will take care of his family." After six months of this incident, Nilakshi's mother also died mysteriously in her home.

After a few months, Manas wrote an article in his office's yearly magazine and narrated the story of Nilakshi. Many of his colleagues appreciated his courage. Since people in Western culture do not believe in such stories, he was able to persuade them through interviews and social media blogs.

There is an existence of a dark world and dark energy, likewise we stay in the world of light. There are many unknown beings which are beyond our visible range. We call them ghosts, spirits, or jinns. These beings possess powers which are beyond our understanding. They are manipulative, and they can see the future and past at the same time. The incident of Manas is one of those thousand stories which many people have experienced in their waking life. But we must warn: do not take these spirits for granted. They follow us like shadows. They get more attracted to beautiful girls, handsome men, strong perfume, alcoholic influences, and extreme rage. There are also many incidents when someone carrying raw meat or fish gets possessed by evil spirits. Our forefathers knew preventive measures, but today's generation is way far from this belief.

Belief in the supernatural is a common part of human life. Although its exact expression varies between individuals and across contexts, some form of belief in spirits, mystic forces, or similar phenomena occurs in nearly every culture. Recently, researchers have been interested in the reasons behind this widespread, seemingly innate human tendency toward supernaturalism for a long time. Many previous studies have examined the psychological and social dimensions of spiritual belief. However, this study offers the first cross-culturally comparative test focusing on how people use supernatural explanations for the natural and social world. This refers to "the attribution of an event to supernatural processes, such as the actions of a god, ancestor spirit, or human magical practitioners, such as a witch or shaman."

A thorough research is important because it could help us better understand the nature of supernatural beliefs and their role in human life. It could maybe even shed some light on the origin of religious thinking.

www.ingramcontent.com/pod-product-compliance
Lightning Source LLC
Chambersburg PA
CBHW050906180626
46814CB00007B/2926